P9-APX-324

When Vera Was Sick

Vera Rosenberry

Henry Holt and Company • New York

Vera was sick.

Jacko and Jilly

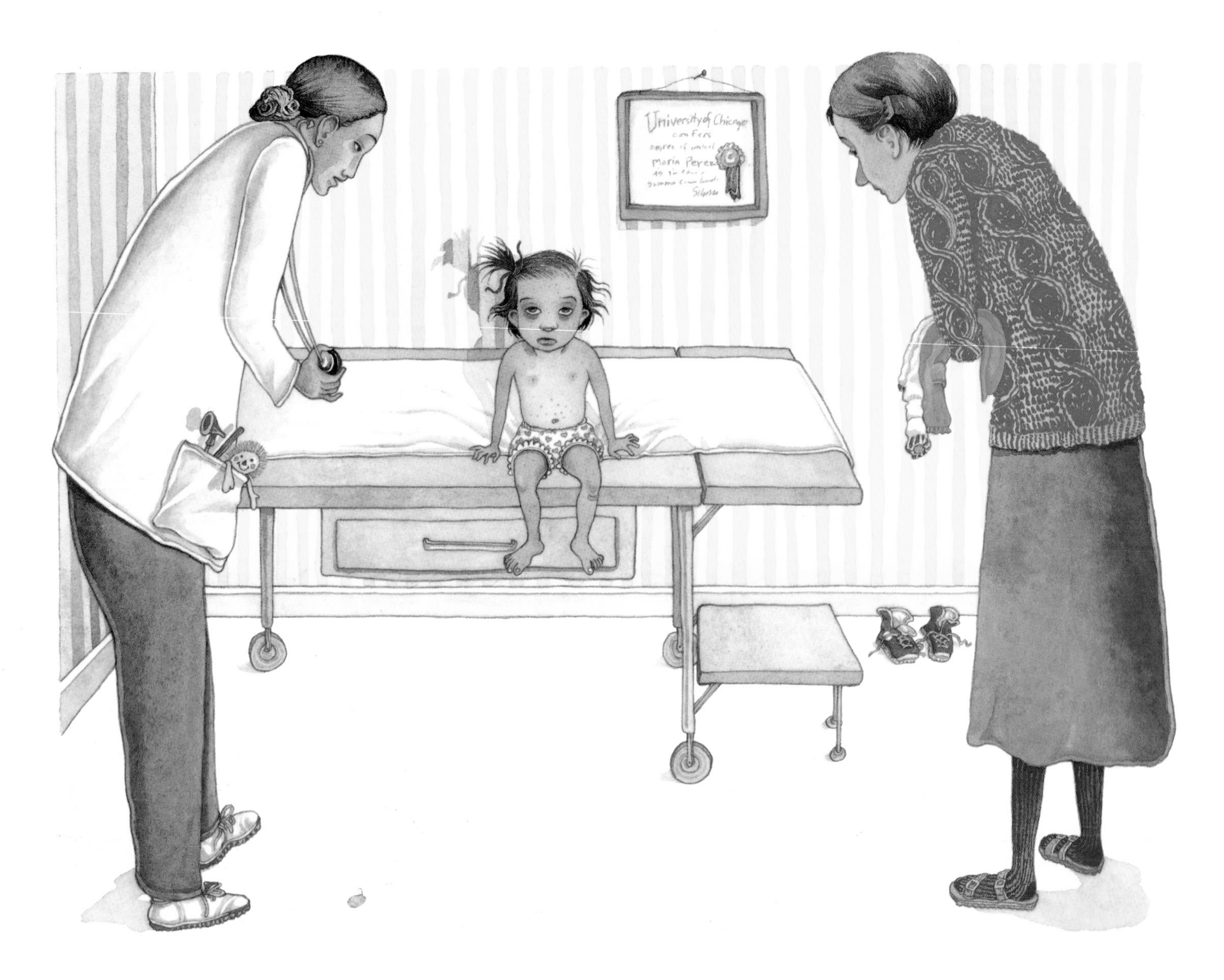

She had spots all over her body, even between her toes and inside her ears.
The doctor said she must stay in bed.

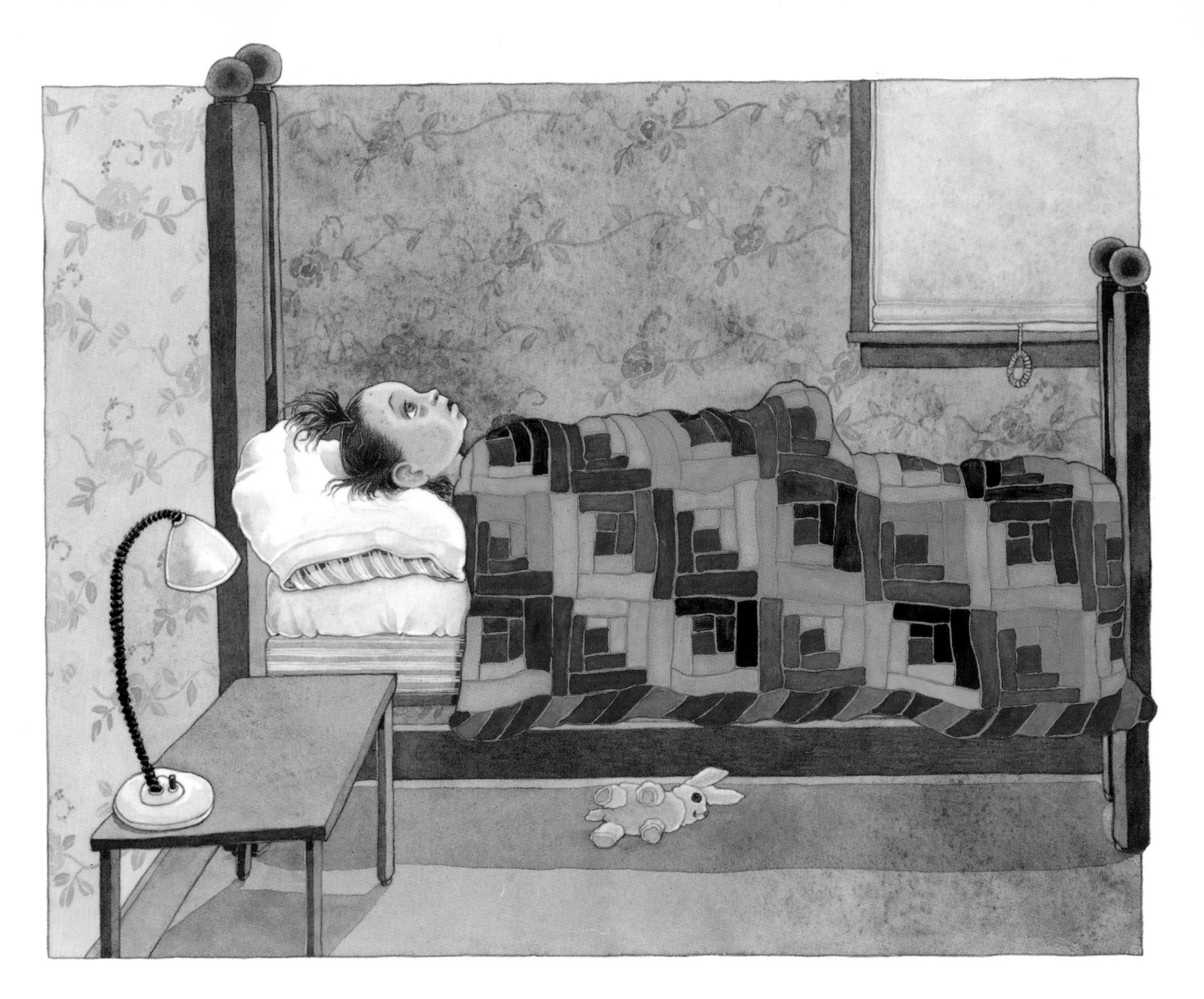

Vera's mother put her in the spare room, away from everyone.
The room was quiet and dark. It was lonely and kind of scary.

Vera was too sick to look at books.

She was too sick to color pictures, even though she had new crayons.

She was too sick to do anything, except scratch her spots.

Big flowers in the wallpaper seemed to bend over Vera's bed.
In deep, spooky voices, they kept saying, "Vera . . . V. e. r. a . . . V . . e . . r . . a. . . ."

“Mom, come quick!” Vera cried. Her tummy ached all over.
Vera’s mother helped her wobble to the bathroom.

Mother brought in the "kitty,"
a big, silky stuffed pillow with arms.
It was used only when someone was sick.

The kitty was warm and soft, like Grandma,
and it smelled good.

Vera sat up and drank some
orange juice through a straw.

Her mother put pink lotion
on all the spots.

She read Vera a story, the one about a little elephant.

“Go to sleep now,” said Mother.
Vera tried.

Talking and laughing voices, clattering and whirring noises came from downstairs. A sweet baking smell drifted into the room.

Slowly . . . carefully . . .
Vera crept downstairs.

Very quietly, she stood in the kitchen doorway.
Mother and June were making gingerbread men.

Sugar

Vera felt hot and dizzy.
She sat down on the floor and scratched her spots.

June saw her.
"Hey, what are you doing here?

YOU'RE SICK!"

Mother gently carried Vera up to the sick room.
She dabbed more calamine lotion on her spots.
"Try to sleep, Vera, and don't scratch."

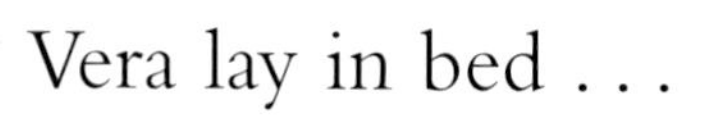

Vera lay in bed . . .

and lay in bed . . .

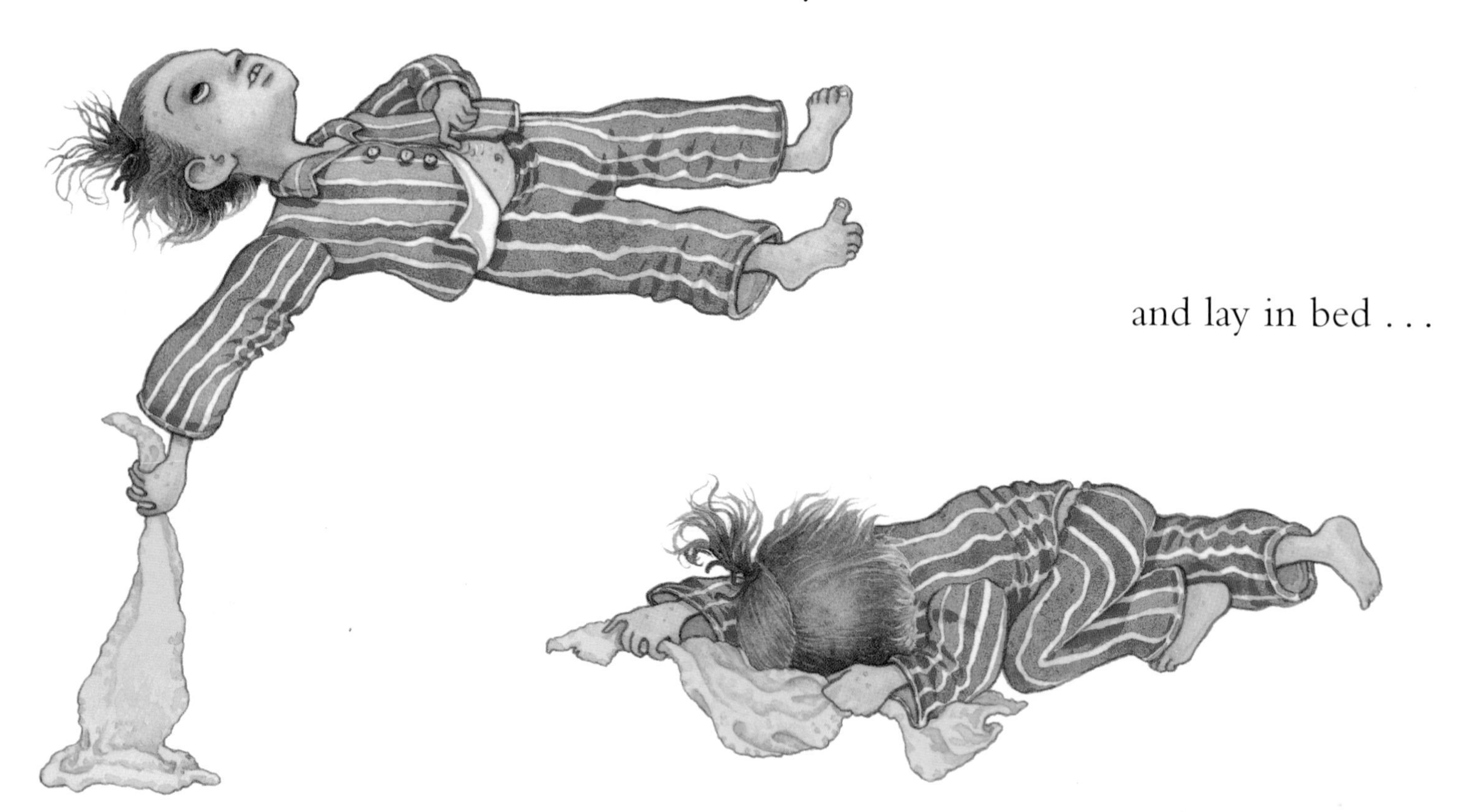

and lay in bed . . .

AND LAY IN BED.

Her spots itched and itched.

After a long time, Vera heard her father's heavy footsteps on the stairs.

He came into the room with a big bouquet of flowers.

Vera could hear everyone
downstairs eating dinner.
Her mother brought up
hot soup on a tray.

Then June practiced the piano for a while.

Vera's father came upstairs to say good night.
He sang "Drink to Me Only with Thine Eyes."

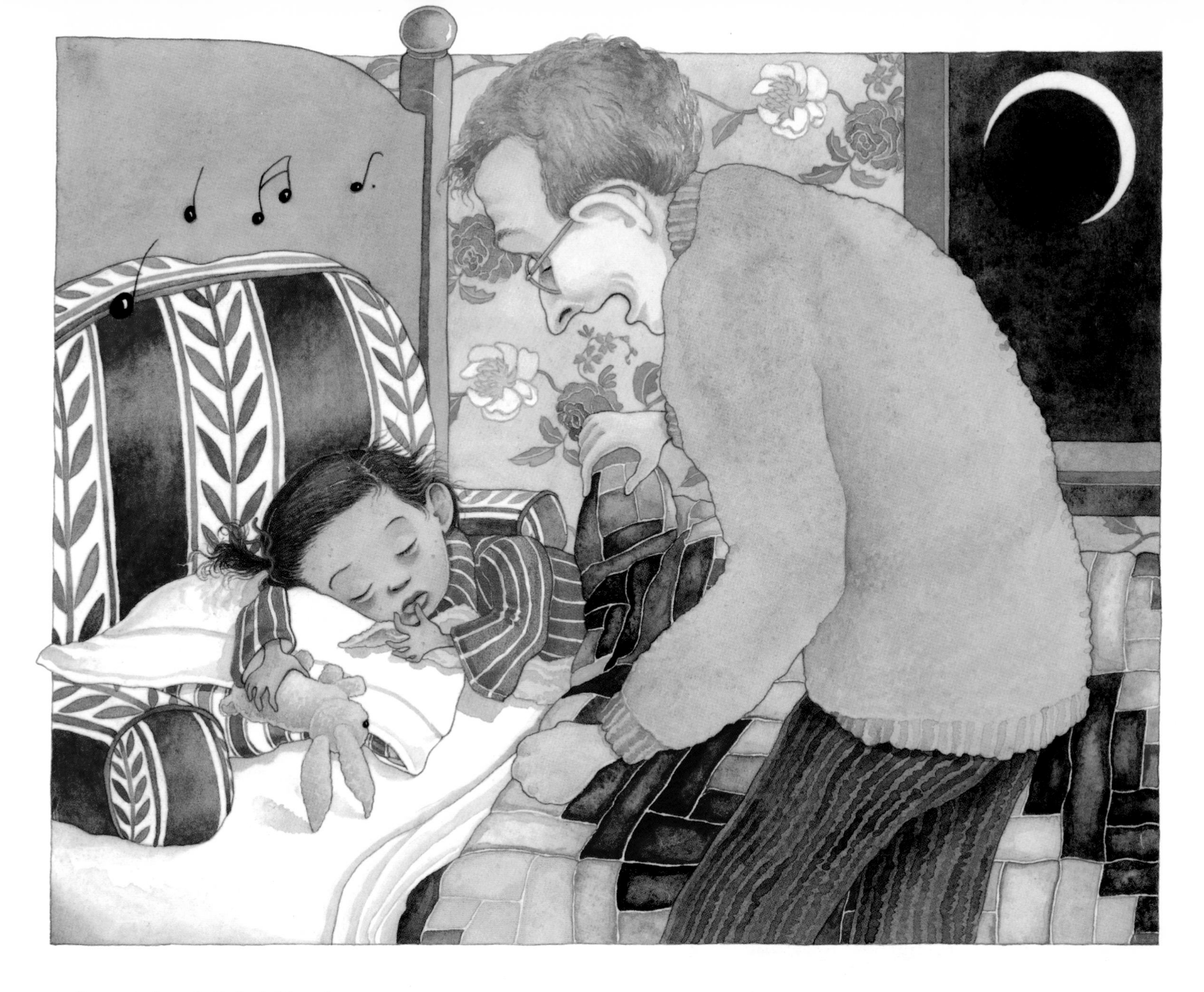

The sick child fell asleep.

Days and nights crawled slowly by.
Vera began to feel better.

She looked at her picture books.
She ate egg custard.
She painted pictures, worked puzzles,
and made many origami animals.

Sometimes June came in and played Chinese checkers with her.

Mother brought out the box
full of old greeting cards.

Vera loved to make up little songs about all the
sheep, snowmen, and perky birds on pine branches.

From her window, Vera watched the other children play outside.
She was tired of being sick.

A few days later, Vera woke up feeling like her old self. Her spots no longer itched, and they were almost gone.

Vera jumped out of bed,

threw off her pajamas, and pulled on her clothes.

She was no longer the sick child.

HOORAY!!

To the memory of my mother and father,
and to June —V. R.

Henry Holt and Company, Inc., *Publishers since 1866*
115 West 18th Street, New York, New York 10011

Henry Holt is a registered trademark of Henry Holt and Company, Inc.

Published in Canada by Fitzhenry & Whiteside Ltd.,
195 Allstate Parkway, Markham, Ontario L3R4T8.

Library of Congress Cataloging-in-Publication Data
Rosenberry, Vera. When Vera was sick / by Vera Rosenberry.
Summary: When spots break out all over her body, Vera must stay in the sickroom
where it is lonely and scary and where she can't fall asleep.
[1. Chicken pox—Fiction. 2. Sick—Fiction.] I. Title. PZ7.R719155Wh 1998 [E]—dc21 97-50442

ISBN 0-8050-5405-7 / First Edition—1998
Typography by Meredith Baldwin
The artist used ink and gouache on Lan Aquarelle paper to create the illustrations for this book.
Printed in the United States of America on acid-free paper.∞
10 9 8 7 6 5 4 3 2 1